Whonk, and Whonk Again

WHONK, AND WHONK AGAIN

Jane Clark Brown

Houghton Mifflin Company Boston   1989

for
my
4
men

Library of Congress Cataloging-in-Publication Data

Brown, Jane Clark.
  Whonk, and whonk again.

  Summary: When Phoebe sets out to discover the source
of the strange "whonk" noise she meets an assortment of
unusual characters that help her in her search.
  [1. City and town life—Fiction.   2. Noise—Fiction]
I. Title.
PZ7.B81418Wh 1989   [E]   88-32812
ISBN 0-395-49211-4

Printed in the United States of America

Y 10 9 8 7 6 5 4 3 2 1

Phoebe sat on the front steps with Mr. Barker in her lap. "We're new here," she said to the little angel on top of their lamppost.

"From the country," she explained to the giant pickle on the roof at the corner.

From beyond the pickle factory came beeps and toots and other strange sounds. Strangest of all was a long, low *whonnk, whonnk*

With Mr. Barker for company, she walked to the factory and peeked around the corner. There was only a sad, paint-spattered man sitting on a box. Scattered around were drawings and chalks.

"Excuse me," she said, "but what is that fearsome animal that goes *whonnk, whonnk*?"

The sad man quickly sketched on the sidewalk. The drawing looked like a lopsided cake with three candles until he put small boats along one layer and wavy blue water marks underneath. With a few more strokes, bright flags waved at either end.

"There," he said. "That is your animal: a ferocious ocean liner."

"An ocean liner!" said Phoebe. "Mr. Barker and I want to see it."

"I'll go with you," he said. "Maybe the passengers will buy my pictures."

They hadn't gone far when an orange plopped in front of them. Then another. And another. It was raining oranges. They ran to hide behind a fruit cart.

"One little worm," said the fruit peddler, "and the lady makes like Babe Ruth."

"This is not a good day," said the peddler with a sigh.

"Come with us," said Phoebe. "We're going to see an ocean liner."

"A giant boat like that carries many people," said the peddler. "They may be wanting nice fruit for their journey."

No sooner had he turned his cart around than they heard a voice shouting, "Help! Help! Baby's caught in the drain."

A woman in a long dress was running back and forth by a hole in a wall.

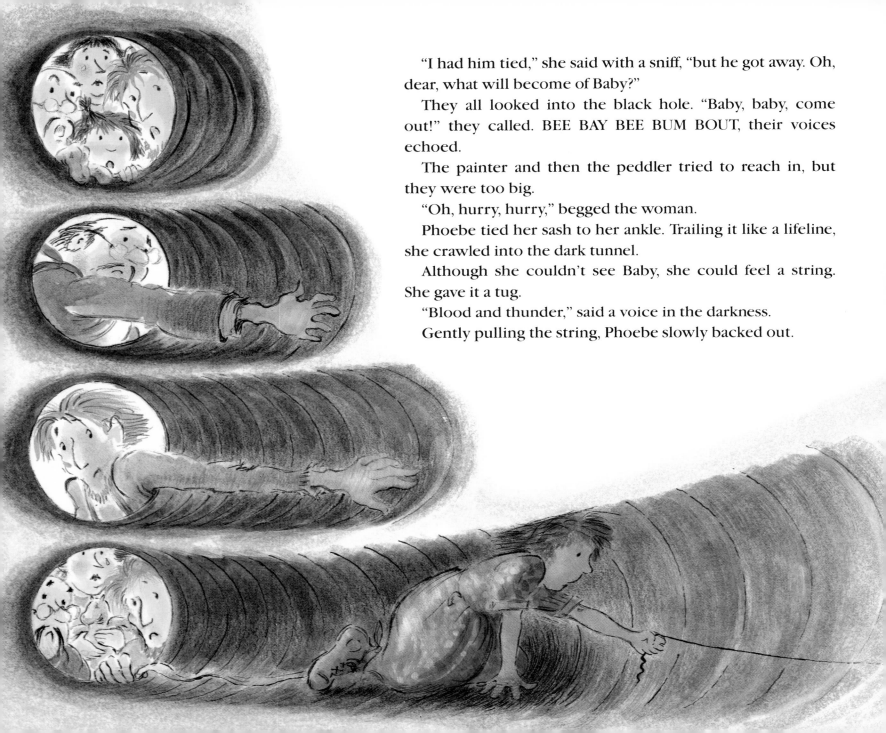

"I had him tied," she said with a sniff, "but he got away. Oh, dear, what will become of Baby?"

They all looked into the black hole. "Baby, baby, come out!" they called. BEE BAY BEE BUM BOUT, their voices echoed.

The painter and then the peddler tried to reach in, but they were too big.

"Oh, hurry, hurry," begged the woman.

Phoebe tied her sash to her ankle. Trailing it like a lifeline, she crawled into the dark tunnel.

Although she couldn't see Baby, she could feel a string. She gave it a tug.

"Blood and thunder," said a voice in the darkness.

Gently pulling the string, Phoebe slowly backed out.

After her came a white cockatoo.

"In your eye," it croaked to its rescuers.

"I want to thank you," the woman said. "Let me tell your special fortune."

"Some other time, if you please," said Phoebe. "We're on our way to an ocean liner."

"An ocean liner! Who knows what you may see there?" said the fortuneteller. "Lovely ladies dancing on the decks, perhaps, or a movie star with his horse.

"Such a grand ship will have many fortune-seekers," she added, putting on her turban. She placed cards and a crystal ball in a basket and led the way into a small park.

When they came out on the other side, their path was blocked by a line of motorcycle policemen.

Phoebe marched right up to one. "We have to get by," she said. "We're going to see the ocean liner."

"Nothing allowed through but parade floats," he said.

Whonk whonk whonk, called the ship's horn.

Suddenly the painter was giving orders to everyone. "Here, hold this. Sit here and tie this around you. Upsy-daisy, little girl. Just wait a moment while I make a sign. Now, we're off to the parade."

They joined the long line of floats that rumbled along the parade route.
"Here comes the Statue of Liberty," someone yelled. People clapped.
"And Justice holding her scales," said another.
"Lookit the real live eagle," shouted a little boy.
"In your eye," said the eagle.

Phoebe enjoyed the view and all the cheering people. Then off to one side she saw a patch of blue water.

"Turn! Turn!" she cried, pointing the banana torch.

"Make way, make way. The Lady goes back to the harbor," said the peddler. He and the painter wheeled the cart onto a side street.

"We should have kept on," grumbled the painter. "We would have won a prize."

"A bigger prize awaits," said the fortuneteller. "The greatest of all ships."

"Are we nearly there?" asked Phoebe.

Before anyone could answer—

two sailors jumped out from behind a fence. The group froze. Only Mr. Barker was not frightened.

Pointing at them from under a cloth were two long shapes like gun barrels.

"Halt! Give us all your money!" the sailors said in angry voices.

"Money, what's money?" said the painter.

The peddler turned out his empty pockets.

"Hand it over!" ordered the first robber.

"Or we'll shoot you!" said the second.

But Phoebe could see the robbers' knees shaking. She gave the cloth a tug. It slipped off, and everyone could see a clarinet and a flute.

The painter and the peddler quickly captured the robbers.

"Oh dear, oh dear," the robbers wailed, taking off their masks.

"We are so hungry," sobbed the flutist.

"And no one will pay to hear us play," cried her twin.

"There now, dears, your fortunes will improve," said the fortuneteller.

"Here, have some fruit, poor things," said the peddler.

"Dry your tears, loves," said the painter, offering his paint rag.

"Come with us," said Phoebe. "We are going to see an ocean liner with dancing ladies. Can you play dance music?"

The twins tweedled a lively tune. The peddler waltzed with the fortuneteller. The painter grabbed Mr. Barker and danced around a lamppost.

"Stop! Stop!" cried Phoebe, pointing toward the bottom of the hill.

"Listen!" said Phoebe. They all listened. Very faintly they heard *whonk whonnk.*

Down they ran to the shining river.

"Look for a floating white palace with tall, leaning smokestacks," said the painter, shading his eyes. "And flags. And thousands of little windows gleaming in the sun."

Phoebe stood on her tiptoes and searched for the giant ship that she wanted to see more than anything in the world.

Toots and honks of work boats mixed with the rattling noises of cranes and loading hoists. And now they heard, louder this time, WHONK WHONK.

"Here it comes!" shouted Phoebe. "I can almost see flags and smokestacks."

They ran to the end of a long wharf.

The twins struck up "The Sailors' Hornpipe." The fortuneteller rubbed her crystal ball and the peddler polished apples. The painter set a canvas on his easel and quickly lettered: WELCOME, LOVELY PEOPLE. PORTRAITS PAINTED WHILE YOU SAIL.

They stared toward the high bridge and waited for the ocean liner.

"It's coming coming coming," chanted Phoebe, hopping up and down.

19

Just then, no more than a stone's throw from the wharf, a tugboat captain pulled his whistle cord. WHONNNK!

"That's no ocean liner," said the painter.

WHONK WHONK! the tug called again, with hoots so loud that the wharf shook.

"No ocean liner?" said Phoebe. She started to cry.

The hornpipe stopped with a two-part squeak.

"Fake! Fake!" the peddler shouted and stomped on his hat.

"Blood and thunder. Blood and thunder," squawked Baby.

The captain turned his tug boat toward the wharf to see what the arguing and weeping was all about.

"You're not an ocean liner," said the fortuneteller. "How dare you sound like one?"

"We were hoping for something larger," said the painter.

"With ladies and a horse," said Phoebe between her snuffles.

"And hungry people," said the fruit peddler.

"All wanting to dance," added the twins.

The captain scratched his head. "No ladies or horses in the cabin today, but if you hop aboard I'll take you to where they can be found."

They looked at the sooty tug. What a grand day for a boat ride! All together they wheeled the fruit cart on board.

The captain let them take turns pulling the whistle cord. Phoebe even touched the steering wheel.

23

The tug docked near a green park. Flags fluttered from a banner that read LEMON STREET FAIR.

"There you are," said the captain. "They've had their parade. They'll be hungry and ready to dance."

"They'll want their fortunes told, too," said one of the twins, "and bright pictures to remember the day by."

"Look, little girl, there's a Ferris wheel," said the other twin. "Would you like a ride on it?"

"No, thank you," said Phoebe. "I can't be late for supper."

"Goodbye then, little girl," said the fruit peddler. He went across the gangplank after the others.

They all waved as Phoebe and the tug started back down the river.

"We didn't see an ocean liner," shouted the painter, "but we had a lovely time."

"Goodbye, goodbye," Phoebe called back. She wondered how she and Mr. Barker would find their way home alone.

The captain left her at the long wharf. "Hurry home, little girl," he said. "It will be dark soon."

At the top of the hill Phoebe stopped to see which way to go. A big hairy dog jumped out at her.

"Go 'way!" she said, and in her fright she dropped Mr. Barker. The dog snatched Mr. Barker and ran off.

"Come back!" Phoebe cried. "Please come back." At each corner the dog sat down and waited for her, but when she was almost close enough to grab Mr. Barker, the dog ran away again.

28

Through darkening streets she ran. In a deserted square
she stopped, turned, and turned again. Big dog and little dog
had both disappeared. She was lost and all alone.

Phoebe didn't know what to do. She felt very, very small.

Suddenly a string of lights raced, one after another, around a giant pickle — her pickle, by her street. She ran until the sign was almost overhead.

There was the lamppost with the little angel on top. Phoebe hurried toward her front steps. In the lamplight a strange shape, a stringy lump, lay on the bottom step.

"Mr. Barker!" she cried and hugged him as hard as she could. Out from behind the trash can came the hairy dog to lick her face. She gave him a big hug, too, because he had brought Mr. Barker home.

Then she tied her sash around his neck and together they climbed the stairs.